Teddy's Birthday

First published in the UK in 2004 by
QED Publishing
A Quarto Group Company
London EClV 2TT
www.qed-publishing.co.uk

Reprinted in this format in 2006

A Catalogue record for this book is available from the British Library.

ISBN 1 84538 564 0

Written by Anne Faundez
Designed by Alix Wood
Illustrated by Karen Sapp

Creative Director Zeta Davies
Senior Editor Hannah Ray

Printed and bound in China

Teddy's Birthday

Anne Faundez

QED Publishing

QED

The toys are up early. What's happening today?
They bump and they bounce; they're ready to play.

Now they are gathered, it's time for some fun.
It's Teddy's birthday; today he is ONE!

"It's my BIRTHDAY!"
cries Teddy,
"I hope everyone's ready!

It's party-time soon,
let's decorate the room!"

Balloons all around, flowers everywhere,
a banner on the wall, streamers in the air.

"Oh wow!" says Teddy.
"Party now! Are you ready?"

They share out the hats in blue, green, and red. Teddy takes TWO to put on his head!

"Let's play some games," say the Twin Yellow Bears.

So they play pass the parcel and musical chairs.

They clap to the music and make lots of noise,
Big Bear, Brown Bear—all of the toys.

Amanda the Panda and Jimmy Giraffe,

together they dance and soon start to laugh.

Fluffy the Bunny has made lots of treats, cookies and cakes, ice cream and sweets.

Everyone's hungry. They each find a seat.
With tummies a-rumbling, they tuck in and eat.

Next, there's a cake on a big silver dish. Teddy blows hard and then makes a wish.

The toys clap their hands and together start singing.
Teddy is happy and cannot stop grinning.

"Happy Birthday to you,
Happy Birthday to you!
Happy Birthday, dear Teddy!
Happy Birthday to you!"

There's a gift for Teddy. He's very excited.

A new bouncy ball!
He's truly delighted!

The toys are now yawning. Such sleepy heads!

They put on pyjamas and climb into bed.

After such an exciting and busy, busy day,

they close their eyes

and fall asleep... straightaway.

Do you remember?

How many hats did
Teddy put on his head?

What shape is
on Teddy's
new ball?

Who made the tasty treats for the toys to eat?

Who is Amanda the Panda dancing with?